Hello, Family Members,

Learning to read is one of the most important ~~~~~~~~~~ nts of early childhood. **Hello Reader!** ~~~~~~~~~~ elp children become skilled readers ~~~~~~~~~~ ing readers learn to read by rememb~~~~~~~~~~ ds like "the," "is," and "and"; by using ~~~~~~~~~~ ew words; and by interpreting picture ~~~~~~~~~~ oks provide both the stories children e~~~~~~~ and the structure they need to read fluently and independently. Here are suggestions for helping your child *before*, *during*, and *after* reading:

Before

- Look at the cover and pictures and have your child predict what the story is about.
- Read the story to your child.
- Encourage your child to chime in with familiar words and phrases.
- Echo read with your child by reading a line first and having your child read it after you do.

During

- Have your child think about a word he or she does not recognize right away. Provide hints such as "Let's see if we know the sounds" and "Have we read other words like this one?"
- Encourage your child to use phonics skills to sound out new words.
- Provide the word for your child when more assistance is needed so that he or she does not struggle and the experience of reading with you is a positive one.
- Encourage your child to have fun by reading with a lot of expression . . . like an actor!

After

- Have your child keep lists of interesting and favorite words.
- Encourage your child to read the books over and over again. Have him or her read to brothers, sisters, grandparents, and even teddy bears. Repeated readings develop confidence in young readers.
- Talk about the stories. Ask and answer questions. Share ideas about the funniest and most interesting characters and events in the stories.

I do hope that you and your child enjoy this book.

— Francie Alexander
Reading Specialist,
Scholastic's Learning Ventures

To my friend
Chuang-chuang

— B. H.

Copyright © 2001 by Nancy Hall, Inc.
All rights reserved. Published by Scholastic Inc.
SCHOLASTIC, HELLO READER, CARTWHEEL BOOKS, and associated logos
are trademarks and/or registered trademarks of Scholastic Inc.

Library of Congress Cataloging-in-Publication Data

Packard, Mary
        The shy scarecrow / by Mary Packard; illustrated by Benrei Huang.
        p. cm. – (Hello reader! Level 1)
        "Cartwheel books."
        Summary: A shy scarecrow is too scared of the hungry crows to do his job, but the
        farmer helps him gain the courage he needs.
        ISBN 0-439-31704-5 (pbk.)
        [1. Scarecrows—Fiction. 2. Fear—Fiction. 3. Crows—Fiction. 4. Stories in rhyme.]
        I. Huang, Benrei, ill. II. Title. III. Series.
        PZ8.3.P125 Sh 2001
    [E]—dc21   2001020481

10 9 8 7 6   02 03 04 05
                        Printed in the U.S.A.   24
                        First printing, September 2001

The Shy Scarecrow

by Mary Packard
Illustrated by Benrei Huang

Hello Reader! — Level 1

SCHOLASTIC INC.

New York   Toronto   London   Auckland   Sydney
Mexico City   New Delhi   Hong Kong

"The corn is high,"
the farmer said.
"It's time to fetch
Rags from the shed."

Back in the shed
Rags heard the crows.
He heard them
in the ripe corn rows.

"Caw!" cried the crows.
"This corn is sweet.
Corn for lunch
can't be beat!"

"I'm scared," cried Rags,
"of that wild mob.
And I'm too shy
to do my job!"

The farmer hung
Rags way up high.
The crows saw Rags
as they flew by.

Rags tried his best
not to show
how scared he was
of every crow.

But down they came.
They didn't care.
It was as if
Rags wasn't there.

"Please," begged Rags. "Please don't come near. You're not supposed to be out here."

"Caw!" cried the crows.
"This corn is sweet.
Corn for lunch
can't be beat!"

Rags gave up and
began to cry.
He couldn't be scary.
He was much too shy.

Back in the shed
the farmer found
a shiny hat
upon the ground.

He placed the hat
on Rags's head.
"Now you can do
your job," he said.

The hat was made
of foil and tin
that clattered and spun
around in the wind.

As it flickered and flashed
with a silvery glow,
Rags felt his courage
begin to grow.

Then all at once
the crows took flight.
"A monster's here!"
they cawed in fright.

"Scat!" cried Rags,
who now felt tall.
"I guess I'm scary
after all!"

"It looks," said Rags,
"like I'm the winner.
Those crows won't be having
corn for dinner!"